Fashion Fairy Princess

Thanks fairy much Catherine Coe!

First published in the UK in 2014 by Scholastic Children's Books
An imprint of Scholastic Ltd
Euston House, 24 Eversholt Street
London, NW1 1DB, UK
Registered office: Westfield Road, Southam, Warwickshire, CV47 0RA
SCHOLASTIC and associated logos are trademarks and/or
registered trademarks of Scholastic Inc.

Text copyright © Scholastic Ltd, 2014
Cover copyright © Pixie Potts, Beehive Illustration Agency, 2014
Inside illustration copyright © David Shephard, The Bright Agency, 2014

The right of Poppy Collins to be identified as the author
of this work has been asserted by her.

ISBN 978 1407 14591 4

A CIP catalogue record for this book is available
from the British Library

Printed and bound by CPI Group (UK) Ltd, Croydon, CR0 4YY
Papers used by Scholastic Children's Books are made
from wood grown in sustainable forests.

1 3 5 7 9 10 8 6 4 2

This is a work of fiction. Names, characters, places,
incidents and dialogues are products of the author's imagination
or are used fictitiously. Any resemblance to actual people, living
or dead, events or locales is entirely coincidental.

www.scholastic.co.uk
www.fashionfairyprincess.com

Fashion Fairy Princess

Catkin

in Jewel Forest

POPPY COLLINS

Dream
Mountain

Jewel Forest

Sparkle
City

Star
Valley

River
Sapphire

Shimmer Island

Glitter Ocean

Welcome to the world of the
fashion fairy princesses! Join Catkin
and friends on their magical adventures
in fairyland.

They can't wait to explore

Jewel Forest!

Can you?

Chapter 1

Catkin fluttered along a high branch
of the sapphire-sycamore tree. The
tree leaves shone in the early morning
sunshine and Catkin couldn't help
but spin in delight as she took in
the beautiful forest. "I'm so lucky
to live here," she said to herself. She
loved Jewel Forest more than anything
else, and flying around it always made
her happy.

She skipped on to the fairy skyway,
a network of glittering bridges that
connected the forest houses, shops and
palace. Each spring the forest fairies
rebuilt the bridges with new leaves. In
fact, it was only last week that Catkin had
been part of the skyway building team.
It had been hard work, but worth all the
effort. The skyway was decorated with

all sorts of different-coloured gems, and Catkin thought it looked better than any other year!

As she flew along, she pulled out her to-do list of fairy errands from her ivy-leaf trouser pocket.

Buy starberry muffins from Blossom's bakery ✔
Hand out sycamore flyers
Glowberry candles

On Catkin's shoulder was a bag full of sycamore seeds. But these weren't just any sycamore seeds. They were extra-special seeds that she'd collected from the very tree she lived in − the sapphire sycamore. Not only did each winged seed have a sapphire at its centre, but with a sprinkling of fairy magic, the seeds could be sent anywhere in Jewel Forest. Catkin had the idea to use them as a new forest messaging service. When they arrived at their destination, they would spin a short message from the sender in the air. Catkin thought it would be a great way to send instant messages around the forest – quicker than fairy-mail! Today her plan was to hand out the seeds so the fairies and creatures of the forest could see them in action.

She also needed to pick up glowberry candles for this evening's Walk in the Woods. Catkin had arranged the walk to celebrate the beauty of the forest, and planned to show everyone all the amazing things that grew there. She fluttered along the skyway and spotted the Cavern Café up ahead. *First I'll stop in for a drink*, she thought. All these chores were thirsty work!

The Cavern Café was set inside a large, hollowed-out branch of an opal-oak tree. It ran almost the whole length of the branch, and was sheltered from wind and rain but open to sunshine and the fresh forest air.

"Hello!" Catkin called out as she fluttered into the café. "My usual, please," she said to the waitress, a ladybird named Poppet. Catkin fluttered up to her favourite spot in the café – a terrace along the top of the branch where she could sit and look out at the forest. She sat down at an acorn-nut table and took out her list again. She began adding things with a beeswax pen when Poppet flew up in front of her.

"I'm dreadfully sorry," Poppet squeaked in her high-pitched ladybird voice, "but we've run out of dandelion milkshake.

Can I get you a different flavour, Catkin? How about honey-pear? Or carrot and berry?"

Catkin frowned. She didn't fancy anything else. The dandelion milkshake always quenched her thirst more than anything else, and it was super-tasty too — sweet and creamy but not too filling. She shook her head, making her red curly hair bounce around her. "I think I'll give it a miss, but thanks, Poppet."

"You could try again tomorrow,"
Poppet suggested. "The problem is we couldn't find a single dandelion in the usual clearing today, but I'm hoping some will grow overnight."

Poppet was right – the magical forest often grew plants very quickly, but it was strange that not one dandelion could be found. Catkin popped her to-do list and pen back in her pocket and fluttered up from the chair. "Thanks, Poppet." The fairy knew that it wasn't just *her* favourite milkshake but one of the café's bestsellers. Many of the fairies and forest creatures would be disappointed that it was off the menu.

Catkin pulled out a sapphire-sycamore seed from her bag. "Before I go, can I give you one of these? It's the newest form of messaging in the forest – with

a sprinkle of fairy-dust, you can send a
message almost instantly to anyone in the
forest!"

Poppet clapped her two front legs
together. "What a great idea! Why don't
you leave a pile here and I can tell
customers about them?"

"That would be fantastic — thanks,
Poppet." Catkin grabbed a handful of the
seeds and passed them to the ladybird. "I'd
better be off now. I'll keep my fingers

crossed you have dandelions back in the café tomorrow!"

Chapter 2

Catkin decided to fly straight to Goldie's Groceries to pick up the glowberry candles. At least then she could tick those off her list. She flew along the fairy skyway that led to the silver-willow tree. Goldie's shop was at the base of the tree, beneath the silver leaves which drooped down like layers of beautiful shimmering curtains.

As Catkin reached the forest floor and

zoomed along past the hedgerows, she heard a chirpy voice call out behind her. "Catkin, can you help?"

The red-headed fairy looked over her shoulder. At first she could see nothing but leaves.

"Who's there?" asked Catkin. For a moment, she wondered if it was a pink tree squirrel playing a trick on her – the squirrels were cheeky animals and liked to joke about.

"It's me!" came a squeak. Catkin fluttered backwards towards a glitterberry bush where the voice seemed to be coming from. "I'm stuck!"

Now that she was closer, Catkin could make out the top of a nut-brown head and pale orange tips of fairy wings sticking out of the bush. "Princess Nutmeg, what *are* you doing?"

Nutmeg was the excitable little sister of Princess Primrose. They both lived in the Tree Palace, a pink diamond-nut tree that was covered in wonderful jewels.

"I was collecting glitterberries. I wanted to surprise Primrose with them. But then my wings got stuck in these stupid branches!"

Catkin chuckled to herself. Although the glitterberries were both beautiful and delicious, they were hard to find and even harder to pick, because the branches were covered in thorns. Trust Nutmeg to try anyway. She loved exploring the forest, but didn't always think about the consequences!

"OK, but don't struggle – you don't want to tear your wings," Catkin told Nutmeg. "Let me help you," She reached in and gently pulled away the branches one by one, taking care to avoid the prickly thorns.

Slowly, Nutmeg was revealed. "Oh, thank you, Catkin!" she cried as she fluttered out of the bush. "I thought I was going to be stuck there all day. Here, you deserve the berries!" Nutmeg held out both hands – they were full of sparkling yellow berries.

Catkin shook her head. "No, you take them back to Primrose — I know how much she loves them."

A smile spread across Nutmeg's freckled face. "Thanks, Catkin, if you're sure! So, where are you going?" she asked.

"I'm off to Goldie's to collect glowberry candles for this evening's Walk in the Woods. Are you coming tonight?"

Nutmeg nodded. "Oh yes, definitely — and Primrose is coming, too. We can't wait!"

"That's great!" Catkin smiled. "The forest is beautiful at this time of year — there's so much to see." She paused, then added, "Actually, there is something you could do. . . Would you mind coming to Goldie's to help me carry the glowberry candles? I think there'll be lots!"

"Yes, of course!" said Nutmeg. Catkin was glad to see Nutmeg was her usual enthusiastic self, despite being stuck in the glitterberry bushes for fairy knows how long. "Ooh, and I can see if Goldie has any purple pears in stock. Primrose and I love them!"

Catkin linked arms with the young fairy and they skipped towards the grocery shop. As they travelled, Nutmeg chattered to Catkin about her day exploring the forest. She'd been playing hide-and-seek with the tree squirrels as well as helping a mother sparrow to collect twigs for a new nest.

Catkin smiled as she approached Goldie's shop, at the base of the silver-willow tree trunk. She was looking

forward to entering the maze of rooms
set into the bark, which were filled with
all sorts of forest goodies. There was a
fruit room and a nut room, but also
a furniture room, a book room and a
candle room. She knew Goldie prided
herself on having everything a fairy could
possibly want.

As they got closer, Catkin frowned.
Usually light spilled out of the little
windows, but every single window was
dark. What's more, the large rectangular
door was shut and had a "Sorry – we're
closed!" sign pinned to it. Catkin didn't
think she'd ever seen the door closed
before. It was always open, welcoming
customers inside!

"That's strange," she said to Nutmeg.
The two fairies fluttered up to the door,
and Catkin gave it a strong *rat-a-tat-tat*.

She pressed a pointy ear to the door, but could hear nothing inside.

Meanwhile, Nutmeg had pressed her nose up against one of the windows. "It's really dark inside. I don't think Goldie's there!" she told Catkin.

Catkin shook her head. "Oh well, I'll have to come back later." She felt a panicky feeling welling up inside her. She hated not being organized, and she *so* wanted the walk to go perfectly that evening.

Catkin took one more look through the window, hoping that Goldie might pop up from behind a cupboard or table, but there was nothing – just darkness. *This is strange,* she thought. *Very strange indeed.*

Chapter 3

"Catkin, Nutmeg, whatever are you doing?"

Catkin spun round and saw their friend Willa zooming towards them, her long black shiny hair billowing out behind her.

"Oh hi, Willa. I was hoping to pick up some glowberry candles for tonight's Walk in the Woods," Catkin explained. "But Goldie's shop is shut!"

Catkin saw the frown beneath Willa's

silky fringe. "That's weird – I thought Goldie's shop was *always* open," she said.

"Not today!" Nutmeg said. "And I wanted to get some purple pears, too!"

"But your walk *is* still going ahead tonight, isn't it?" Willa asked Catkin. "I've been looking forward to it for ages!"

"Oh, yes." Catkin nodded, feeling pleased that all her friends were excited about the walk too. "It's just that I *really* wanted those candles for it – they're perfect for walks because they don't go out in the breeze." She looked down, unable to hide her disappointment.

Willa put an arm around Catkin. "Why don't you come with me to What a Gem?" she said. "I was on my way there to check out the new charm bracelets. I guarantee a bit of shopping will cheer you up!"

"But I still have some chores to finish. . ." Catkin began.

"There'll be time for chores later." Willa widened her dark brown eyes. "Oh, come on, Catkin – shopping is always much more fun when there are two of you!"

"Oh . . . OK then," said Catkin. Perhaps she could pick up a new pair of gemstone studs. And maybe some star-shaped diamonds to match the star-print tunic she'd planned to wear on tonight's walk. "Nutmeg, do you want to come too?" Catkin asked the princess.

Nutmeg shook her head, her choppy nut-brown hair swinging about her shoulders. "Jewellery's not really for me – apart from princess tiaras of course!" She winked. "And I should take these glitterberries back to the palace. Primrose will be so pleased!" With that the adventurous little fairy fluttered off, a basket of glitterberries hooked over her shoulder, and her orange wings beating steadily.

Willa took hold of Catkin's hand and the two fairies flew along the skyway towards What a Gem. The shop was in a much higher part of the forest, so they had to criss-cross up some steep bridges to get there.

"Here we are!" announced Willa, pushing open the door of the jewellery shop with one shoulder. Catkin followed her in, but

Willa stopped suddenly in the doorway. "Where *is* everything?"

Catkin looked around. She didn't come in here very often, but she was pretty sure it didn't usually look like this. The windows were bare, the shelves were almost empty, and even the jewellery tree in the centre of the shop had just a couple of necklaces hanging from it.

"Hi, fairies." A large emerald-green

dragonfly emerged from the shadows at the back of the shop and waved. "I'm terribly sorry, but I don't have much today. You see, I haven't had my usual delivery of jewels."

Catkin stepped back in surprise. Jewel Forest was full of jewels – why hadn't there been a delivery?

"Do you think it's just late?" asked Willa.

"Perhaps," said the dragonfly, "but the jewel moths always bring them first thing in the morning, and so far there hasn't been any sign of them. It might be better to try again tomorrow – hopefully they'll turn up then!"

"That's so unlike the jewel moths," said Catkin. The moths that collected the jewels in the forest were always very reliable. "I wonder what's wrong."

Willa and Catkin waved goodbye to

the dragonfly and left What a Gem. Willa looked over her shoulder at the empty window display as they left. "What bad luck!" she said. "Catkin, I think I'm going to head to Starlight-Starbright tailor's and see if they have anything there. I know they sometimes sell accessories too, as well as designing and mending clothes. Do you want to come with me?"

But Catkin was only half listening to her friend. The other half of her brain was busy worrying about the strange things happening in the forest.

"Catkin?" Willa asked again, putting a hand on her arm.

"Oh, sorry, Willa." Catkin shook her head. "Um, no – you go ahead without me. I need to do some investigating." Catkin had a horrible feeling that these things were more than just a coincidence – and she was determined to get to the bottom of it.

Chapter 4

Alone on the skyway, Catkin paused for
a moment. First the dandelions, then
Goldie's shop being shut, and now the
missing jewel delivery. It couldn't all just
be unlucky – she was sure something
strange was going on. *But what can I do?*
she wondered as a wave of worry washed
over her.

She looked around her at the forest,
and the cherry-jewel tree up ahead

caught her eye. Something didn't look
right. The jewels seemed dull, even in
the spring sunshine. She fluttered over
to a branch and hovered in the air. She
touched the cherries that clustered on
the leaves, examining them carefully. No,
they definitely weren't glittering like
usual.

"Hey, Catkin, are you collecting cherry-
jewels?" came a voice from below. Catkin

looked down. It was the pink furry shape of Conker, one of the tree squirrels.

"Hi, Conker. Actually no — there's something wrong with them. In fact, there seems to be something wrong with a lot of the forest."

"Funny you should say that," said Conker. "We've been getting complaints about our daisy-nuts." The tree squirrels collected the tasty nuts to supply the whole of Jewel Forest. "Fairies have been saying they're bitter — not at all sweet and rich like usual."

"Really?" Catkin fluttered down to Conker.

The squirrel nodded and his furry pink tail bounced about. "I don't understand. They've never tasted bad before. Here, try one."

Conker reached into a sack hooked

on to the end of his tail and held out a shiny white nut. Catkin plucked it up and popped it into her mouth. She couldn't help but screw up her face as she chewed. The nut tasted sharp and bitter – not at all like usual. "Oh dear," she said once she'd swallowed.

"I've got to go," said Conker. "I promised Sycamore I'd play acorn-ball with him. But if you find out what's wrong, please let me know."

Catkin nodded as Conker scampered away up a tree trunk. She watched him go, wondering what to do.

"I know," she said to herself after a while, "I'll go and visit the Jewel Tree!" The Jewel Tree was the first tree ever to grow in the forest and the source of all forest fairy magic. It was the most special and powerful tree in the whole of Jewel Forest. If there was a problem, Catkin was sure the tree could help solve it. She beat her red wings hard as she took off and began flying through the forest, focused on reaching it as quickly as she could.

The Jewel Tree was tucked away in a magical corner. Catkin liked to visit

it when she wanted to feel cl
the forest, but as she flew alon
speed, she realized she'd been s
lately that she couldn't remember the
last time she'd been there. As she went
further and further into the forest, away
from the fairy homes, shops and cafés,
she suddenly had a bad feeling, and her
stomach bubbled with worry as she got
closer to the clearing where the tree
grew.

Catkin was almost there when she
turned a corner . . . and gasped. She shut
her eyes, then opened them again, not
wanting to believe what she saw. But it
didn't change. In front of her was not
a beautiful tree glittering with bright
jewels, but a drooping dull tree with
wilting leaves!

The forest fairy collapsed to the

mossy floor. Even the ground — usually
a healthy bright green — was a murky
brown colour. Catkin put her head in

her hands and fought back tears. If the Jewel Tree was dying, then the whole of her beloved Jewel Forest was in danger! She picked herself up and flew over to the trunk of the Jewel Tree. Usually a bright sparkling pink, it was now a pasty grey colour. She wrapped her arms around it, but knew that the love of one fairy wouldn't be enough to fix the special tree.

As she hugged the trunk, Catkin looked up. The branches were usually weighed down with thousands of gems, but today she couldn't see one jewel on the branches. What's more, sparkling fairy-dust usually floated around the trunk and branches, but now there wasn't even a speck of it.

"I'm so sorry," she whispered to the tree. "We've all been taking magic from you, and not giving anything back. I just hope I haven't realized too late."

Chapter 5

Catkin knew that without the Jewel Tree, the entire forest would be doomed. They needed its magic to keep everything growing!

She gave the Jewel Tree trunk one last hug, then stepped away. "I'll be back, I promise," she said. It felt a bit silly talking to a tree – but after all, the tree was alive, just like the fairies and other creatures of the forest were. She looked up at the wilting bare branches and her heart felt like a stone in her chest. She had to act fast, or the Jewel Tree wouldn't be alive for much longer!

Catkin took a deep breath and fluttered upwards into the air. She beat her wings and zoomed back through the forest, towards her home in the sapphire-sycamore tree.

As she fluttered along the fairy skyway, Catkin spotted a familiar figure up ahead. It was her little friend Pip, sitting on a branch outside her tiny tree house in the opal-oak tree. Pip's home was small, to match her size, but very pretty, made from knotted beams that were studded with rubies.

Pip looked up with a smile. "Hi, Catkin! I came to see if you needed any help for tonight's walk. I'm really excited

about it!" Her dark brown eyes twinkled
in the afternoon sunshine.

Catkin felt terrible. Everyone was
looking forward to the walk, but they
didn't know the forest was in trouble.
How could the walk go ahead now?

Pip saw the worry in Catkin's eyes.
"Whatever's wrong, Catkin?" The small fairy
fluttered up and put an arm around her friend.

"It's the Jewel Tree," Catkin began.
"It's . . . it's dying!"

Pip's forehead creased in a deep frown.
"What? What do you mean?"

Catkin pointed at a branch of the
opal-oak tree. "Do you notice anything
different about the opal jewels?"

Pip squinted at the jewels that hung on
the leaves. "Hmm. Well, now you mention
it, they do look rather dull. And there
aren't half as many as usual. What's going
on?"

"It's not just this tree – it's everywhere in the forest. First there were no dandelions for the milkshakes at the Cavern Café this morning, then Goldie's Groceries was closed. I went to What a Gem with Willa, and it hadn't had its usual delivery of jewels – in fact, it had almost run out. I think I know why. We haven't been looking after the forest, and the Jewel Tree is in a bad way – I'm worried it might be dying!"

Pip immediately felt guilty. Only yesterday, she had been picking gooseberries for a tart, not even thinking about whether the bush she'd emptied would be able to grow more. "This is terrible." She slumped back down on the branch and sighed.

"I've got to work out a way to fix it," said Catkin. "There must be something I can do."

Pip looked up at her friend. "But this isn't a one-person problem, Catkin — I know you're great at getting things done, but you can't sort this out by yourself."

"You're right!" said Catkin, her spirits lifting slightly as the beginnings of an idea started to form in her head. "I'll call an emergency meeting at Toadstool Town Hall. I'll get everyone to come. The whole forest will want to help!"

"Yes, that would be a great start!" said Pip. "I can help spread the message about the meeting if you like? I'm not the fastest flyer, but I'll do as much as I can."

Catkin shook her head. "No need!" She slung the bag off her shoulder and pulled out a sapphire-sycamore seed. "We can use these!"

She explained to Pip how they worked, and the two fairies were soon sprinkling fairy-dust on the seeds. With each seed containing a message about the emergency meeting, they sent them spinning off into the air to every single fairy and creature in the forest.

Seconds later, in the Tree Palace, a sapphire-sycamore seed floated through a leaf-shaped window into Princess Primrose's huge circular bedroom.

"What's that?" said Nutmeg, who was helping Primrose pin her hair into a French plait, ready for the walk that evening.

Instead of falling to the wooden floor, the seed began spinning about the room, and the sisters stared at it. As it moved, fairy-dust flew from the seed and spelt out a sparkly message in the air:

Urgent! Please come to an emergency
meeting at 'Toadstool Town Hall at noon
today.
Thank you.
Catkin x

"An emergency meeting?" said Nutmeg
as she watched the magical dust float
slowly to the floor and the message
disappear.

Primrose frowned. "That doesn't sound
good." She glanced up at the pink cuckoo
clock on her wall. "Oh, look, it's almost
noon – we'd better hurry!"

The two sisters dropped the hairpins on
Primrose's dressing table and flew out of
the bedroom, all thought of French plaits
forgotten. Nutmeg whispered into the
fairy-ear-shaped knot in the wall outside,
which slid away to reveal a secret passage –

the quickest way to get in and out of
the palace. Holding hands, they zoomed
along the skyway towards the town hall,
worrying all the way what the emergency
was and whether Catkin was OK.

Chapter 6

In Toadstool Town Hall, Catkin waited
anxiously on the centre stage for
everyone to arrive. What if the sycamore
seeds hadn't worked? There was no time
to lose — they needed to do something
to save the forest right away! Pip stood
at the door and, to Catkin's relief,
was soon ushering in hordes of fairies,
forest animals and creatures. Everyone
had concerned looks on their faces,

and although she didn't want to panic
everybody, Catkin was glad to see they'd
taken her emergency meeting seriously.
I really hope this works, she thought to
herself as she waved at the fairies and
creatures coming in.

The town hall was one of the most
impressive buildings in the forest. On
either side of the entrance stood two
golden statues – one of a princess fairy

and one of a hummingbird. They were there to show how the fairies and creatures of the forest always lived and worked together in harmony. The circular walls were built of amber gemstones, and let in the sunshine from outside without the need for windows. The hall was filled with red-and-white toadstools, which the fairies and creatures now sat on, looking up at Catkin expectantly.

She suddenly felt very nervous. She hadn't prepared what she wanted to say, and although she loved organizing things, she didn't really like speaking in front of a big audience!

Catkin felt a tug at her elbow. She turned to see Pip beside her. "I think that's everyone," she said in her little voice.

"What am I going to say?" whispered Catkin, feeling jittery with panic.

Pip gave her a small smile. "Just be yourself," she said. "Everyone will soon see how important it is to save the Jewel Tree."

"Thanks, Pip," said Catkin, pushing her red curly hair behind her pointy ears and taking the bellflower microphone in her hand. She thought back to the sight of the wilting Jewel Tree and how much it needed their help, and began to speak.

"Thank you for coming today at such short notice," she said in a slightly shaky voice. "I wouldn't have asked you all here if it wasn't a real emergency." Catkin breathed in deeply,

preparing to break the news to everyone. "Some of you may have noticed that the forest hasn't been as magical as usual lately. Plants and flowers have stopped growing, and the jewels are dull and disappearing."

Catkin paused and looked out over the audience. She saw some nodding heads, and everybody had worried looks on their faces.

"I went to visit the Jewel Tree today and . . . well, it looked terrible, with not one jewel on its branches."

Catkin heard everyone gasp as they took in the news. She hated to shock everyone, but she needed their help.

"I hope it can be rescued," she continued, "but we need to start looking after our beautiful home. We've been taking lots from it but giving nothing back, and the Jewel Tree is dying. Will you help me?"

She glanced up hopefully, and shouts filled the hall: "Yes!" "Of course!" and "What can we do!"

Thank fairyness, thought Catkin. It seemed as if everyone was willing to help.

"Let's go to the Jewel Tree. We need to start there – to give back its magic. Follow me!"

With that Catkin flapped her red wings and zoomed from the stage and out of the town hall. She looked over her shoulder and saw that every single fairy and creature in the hall had already jumped up from their toadstool and was heading towards the arched doorway. Catkin let out a little sigh of relief. Now she just hoped her plan would work!

Catkin reached the Jewel Tree first and waited at the trunk for the rest of the forest to arrive. Fairies fluttered down to land on the brown mossy ground, gasping as they took in the awful sight of the dying tree.

"What have we done?" said Willa quietly, her eyes brimming with tears. "I feel awful, neglecting the forest like this."

Her fairy friend Blossom came up

beside her. "Poor forest. No wonder I've been having trouble getting all my cake ingredients. I didn't stop to think that something serious might be wrong."

Goldie nodded her head, her tight blonde curls bouncing up and down as she did so. "I closed my grocery shop because I'd run out of everything, but I thought it would get better. I didn't realize we'd been treating the forest so badly."

Soon, everyone who lived in the forest had arrived at the Jewel Tree. *They all look horrified,* thought Catkin. *Even the cheeky tree squirrels.* The pink squirrels had grouped around the base of the tree, staring at the dull trunk, tears running down their fluffy faces.

Butterflies hovered in the air, shocked at the sight of the tree, and birds circled slowly above. Frogs and toads sat on their haunches, silent, while ants and beetles stopped their marching. The forest fairies all stood frozen, their mouths gaping open.

Pip tapped Catkin on the shoulder. "This is just dreadful. I hadn't imagined

the tree would look quite as bad as this.
But what in fairyland can we do?"

Chapter 7

Catkin clapped her hands together to gather everyone's attention. The fairies and creatures all turned their eyes on her, waiting to hear what she was going to say. It made her nervous, but she was determined.

"I know the Jewel Tree looks terrible – but I think we can save it!" she began. "What it needs is love and a bit of fairy magic. We should at least try!" Catkin pulled out a handful of fairy-dust from her pocket and held her fist in the air. "Let's use all the fairy-dust we have and sprinkle it over the Jewel Tree."

As everyone watched, Catkin fluttered to the very top of the tree and scattered every last speck of fairy-dust over the wilting branches.

"And we can plant jewels around its base to help it grow again." Catkin took a sapphire-sycamore seed out of her bag, dug a shallow hole in the ground with her hands and laid the seed inside. Then she pushed back the soil to fill in the hole. "With all of us helping, we can put some magic back into its roots to save it. Who's willing to try?"

Every single fairy and forest creature held up a hand, paw, leg or wing.

Catkin smiled. "Then let's start right away!"

Fairies began flying to the top of the Jewel Tree and emptying their pockets of fairy-dust over it, just like Catkin had done. Pip zoomed up and took fistfuls of dust from her denim dungarees. She brought them up to her face and whispered, "Get better, Jewel Tree, please!"

Meanwhile, some of the fairies were flying back to their tree houses to collect more fairy-dust. Every fairy had a stash at home, to pay for shopping and help with magic around the forest, but they didn't mind giving every sprinkle of their dust to the tree – not if it would help save it.

The forest creatures were running and scampering about, collecting jewels that could be planted around the base of the tree. "We'll dig up all the emerald nuts we've hidden!" Conker told Catkin. "And we'll bring them back here to plant. We tree squirrels must have buried thousands of nuts around the forest!"

"Thank you," said Catkin. "That will be a big help, I'm sure."

Everyone worked together. Sparrows and magpies searched for dropped jewels on the forest floor with their beaks. Each time they found one, the ants carried it back to the tree. For tiny insects, they were super-strong, able to manage even conker-sized gems on their backs. At the tree, rabbits and hares dug holes for the jewels to be

dropped in, then covered them over when
they'd been filled with gems.

All Catkin's fairy friends worked very
hard, too. Primrose and Nutmeg had
flown back to the Tree Palace to collect
as much fairy-dust as they could find.
She soon saw them flying back carrying a
shiny red chest between them.

"It's royal fairy-dust from the palace
cellar," Nutmeg told Catkin excitedly.
"This chest is full of it! Come on – let's
pour it over!"

Primrose smiled at her little sister.

"Make sure you're very careful — it's really heavy and we don't want to spill it before we get to the tree."

"Here, let me help," Willa offered. She flew to the top of the Jewel Tree with the two sisters and opened the lid while Primrose and Nutmeg tipped the chest over. A thick cloud of sparkling fairy-dust floated down, covering every single drooping branch.

Over in a leafy part of the forest, Blossom and Pip flew about, helping the jewel moths look for gems that could be buried around the tree. "Here's some!" cried Blossom, diving down to the base of a cherry-jewel tree where lots of red jewels lay fallen on the ground. She began stuffing them in the pockets of her daisy-petal shorts, but the pockets were small and she couldn't squeeze many in.

"Wait a minute," said Pip in her little voice. "Let's ask the beetles to take back the jewels for us — then we can go looking for more."

Blossom slapped a hand to her forehead. "Why didn't I think of that? Great idea!"

Soon hundreds of beetles were marching back to the Jewel Tree, each carrying a cherry-jewel on their back,

while Blossom and Pip went in search
of more.

Catkin stayed near the tree, making sure
the fairy-dust and jewels were scattered
evenly, and giving jobs to fairies and
creatures who weren't sure what to do.
The tree hadn't changed at all yet, not
as far as she could see, but Catkin tried
not to be disappointed – she thought
it might take some time for the fairy-
dust and jewels to work. She hoped so,
anyway, from the bottom of her heart.

As she looked up to watch Willa scatter
more fairy-dust over the tree, she noticed
the sky had turned a light purple. It was
dusk – the sun was setting! They wouldn't
be able to work for much longer. But
Catkin had one more idea up her sleeve.

As the crescent moon rose in the sky,
Catkin gathered everyone round. "Thank
you for everything you've done," she said.
"You've all worked so incredibly hard. I
have one last idea to help save the Jewel
Tree – and our forest."

The fairies and creatures glanced
around at one another. What else could
they possibly do?

"Each and every one of us lives in the
forest, and we're a big part of what makes
it special and magical. So I'm going to
stay here and sleep next to the Jewel Tree
tonight to show the forest just how much

I love it. Who will stay with me?"

"Me! Me! Me!" everyone shouted at once.

What a good idea, thought Blossom.

"A camping sleepover? Brilliant!" said Nutmeg, jumping up and down.

Catkin was delighted when every single fairy and creature agreed to join her. They all began to set up camp. The fairies made tents of leaves and beds of moss while the animals dug burrows. The birds made nests out of twigs, and the butterflies found shelter in the nearby hedgerows.

As the stars twinkled in the inky-black sky, everyone settled down for the night. In the tent Catkin shared with her friends, Willa began whistling the sacred forest fairy song. Soon everyone joined in – even the worms and the beetles. They sang gently, hoping the song would be

another thing to help heal the Jewel Tree.

Catkin snuggled up under her mossy
blanket. If the Jewel Tree hadn't been in
such danger it would have been a magical
evening, but all she could think about
was whether they'd done enough to save
the tree. Catkin was so worried she didn't
think she would ever get to sleep. But
she'd worked so hard that day, and felt
her eyelids getting heavier and heavier.

Eventually she drifted off to sleep as the birds sang lullaby tweets. In the morning, they'd find out whether they'd done enough to save the Jewel Tree. For now, the forest slept.

Chapter 8

Catkin blinked in the sunlight that streamed into the tent and rubbed her eyes with the balls of her hands. She looked around at her friends – all still sound asleep on their mossy beds. She crawled out of the leaf-tent and looked up at the sky, expecting to see rays of bright sunshine.

"Oh my fairyness!" she cried. It wasn't the sun that shone in her eyes – the sky was still dark and the moon still out. It was the sparkling Jewel Tree! "Pip, Willa, Blossom! Primrose, Nutmeg! Come and look!"

The mossy
blankets
rustled as
the fairies
threw back the
covers. "Wow!"
squealed Nutmeg.
"It's a miracle!"

"We did it!" cried Blossom.

The fairies stared up at the tree in awe, huge beams on their faces.

Catkin had to agree with Princess Nutmeg. It did seem like a miracle. She'd never seen the Jewel Tree look so magical. The tree trunk was back to its glittering pink colour and the branches no longer drooped. Instead, they rose upwards, covered in shining leaves and thousands of different-coloured jewels. The sparkling fairy-dust covered every branch, leaf and jewel, and fairy magic glistened all over the tree. In fact, Catkin could *feel* the magic buzzing from it, giving her goosebumps on her arms.

As the fairy friends took in the transformed Jewel Tree, the sun peeped over the horizon, and the rest of the forest began waking up. The birds tweeted in excitement at the sight of the tree, then started a beautiful dawn chorus.

Every fairy gasped when they woke and saw the Jewel Tree looking so wonderful again. They were soon fluttering about, staring at its incredible beauty and the magic, oohing and aahing at the ancient tree.

But Catkin couldn't relax — not quite.

She knew how important it was never to let anything like that happen again. She fluttered to the base of the tree and the fairies and forest creatures all turned to face her.

"We saved the Jewel Tree – and the forest!" she said loudly and clearly, realizing that for the first time she didn't feel nervous about speaking to a crowd. "But from now on, every fairy and creature here – no matter how small – must take care of our magical home. We've got to look after it, and not take anything for granted. We must promise never to neglect the Jewel Tree and the forest again."

"We promise!" everyone replied in unison. The clearing was filled with the sound of fairies and creatures all applauding and cheering.

"Can we have a party to celebrate?" asked Nutmeg, a cheeky smile on her freckled face.

Primrose put an arm around her sister. "I've got a better idea – and one that means we don't need to take anything from the forest. How about the Walk in the Woods we didn't get to do yesterday?"

"Oh yes — that would be perfect!" said Blossom.

Catkin frowned. "But I'm not ready — and I don't have the candles!" She didn't like to do anything unless she was properly prepared.

"But we don't need candles — not in the daytime," said Willa, pointing to the rising sun in the blue sky.

"And it really would be the perfect celebration," added Pip.

Catkin smiled at her best friends. "You're right. Let's do it!"

The red-headed fairy announced the plan to the rest of the forest and moments later, everyone had gathered round her, ready for the walk to begin. "We'll start with the most special thing in Jewel Forest," said Catkin. "The Jewel Tree!"

All the forest fairies and creatures followed in a long line as Catkin began the Walk in the Woods. First she carefully touched the sparkling pink bark of the Jewel Tree and explained that it was thousands of years old. "Legend says that it grew from the seed of a diamond, which had been dropped by a magical unicorn. Long ago, a group of fairies discovered the magical tree and decided to make their home here."

Catkin took them around the Jewel Tree clearing, then led everyone towards the River Sapphire. "The river runs all the way through fairyland," she said. "Not only is it great for swimming and sailing, but it gives essential water and life to the forest, and is a wonderful home for all the water-loving creatures." Catkin grinned as she spoke. She loved

talking about Jewel Forest, and now
everyone had helped save it, it felt
extra-special.

As the Walk in the Woods party
travelled back towards the main part
of the forest, where the fairies all
lived, Catkin pointed out the different
hedgerows and trees. "See those bushes
over there? They're glitterberry bushes –
and they have very sharp thorns. Take

special care if you want to pick the berries — and only gather a few at a time." She winked at Nutmeg.

"I've learnt my lesson — I promise!" the fairy princess told Catkin.

"And these are poppy-petunias," Catkin said as they passed a mass of red-and pink speckled flowers that covered the forest floor like a giant blanket. "They don't grow anywhere else but here in Jewel Forest."

"They're beautiful," said Willa. She'd never paid much attention to all the things that grew in the forest, but now she was fascinated by it all.

Catkin soon reached the fairy skyway and began fluttering along the bridges. She continued explaining more about the forest as the fairies and creatures followed behind.

"Wow – we're so lucky to live here!" said Blossom as the walk came to an end outside the Cavern Café.

Everyone crowded into the café and started ordering drinks. Catkin was delighted to find the dandelion milkshake was back on the menu!

"Thanks for a wonderful walk." Primrose came up to Catkin and squeezed her in a hug. "It was like one big travelling party!"

"It really was, wasn't it?" said Catkin. She held up her acorn cup and made a toast. "To our wonderful forest!"

Every fairy and forest creature raised

their glasses and beamed. "To the forest!" they all replied.

"And to Catkin!" added Primrose. "For showing us just how special it is."

"To Catkin!" everyone shouted together.

Catkin's heart felt as if it would burst with happiness now that they'd saved the forest. She knew that no one would forget just how lucky they were to all live here — and the Jewel Tree would never be in danger again.

If you enjoyed this

Fashion Fairy Princess

book then why not visit our
magical new website!

- Explore the enchanted world of
the fashion fairy princesses
- Find out which fairy princess
you are
- Download sparkly screensavers
- Make your own tiara
- Colour in your own picture frame
and much more!

fashionfairyprincess.com

Fashion Fairy Princess

Pip

in Jewel Forest

Turn the page for a sneak peek of the next
Fashion Fairy Princess adventure...

Chapter 1

Toadstool Town Hall in Jewel Forest
hummed with the chatter of fairies as
they waited for the meeting to begin.
The town hall was an impressive circular
building deep in the magical forest. The
walls were made entirely of gemstones,
which let light flow in from outside, even
though there were no windows.

Pip, Willa, Catkin and Blossom sat next
to each other on red-and-white toadstool

seats, waiting for someone to appear on the stage in the centre of the hall.

"I wonder what this is all about," said Willa as she adjusted her sycamore hairband in her long dark hair. "I hope there isn't something wrong in the forest!"

"Maybe it's something good," Pip said in her tiny fairy voice. Pip was the smallest of all of her friends, and she had a voice to match.

"Well, it can't be a celebration," added Blossom, who owned the bakery in Jewel Forest, "because I haven't been asked to bake a special cake!"

"Oh look, it's the mayor," whispered Catkin. She nodded her head at the stage, making her red curly hair bounce about.

A large yellow frog hopped along one of the aisles and on to the stage. He wore a smart red waistcoat that sparkled with ruby jewels.

Ribbit, he said into the bellflower microphone on the stage. "Is this microphone working?" *Ribbit!*

The audience was a sea of bobbing heads as everyone nodded at the same time.

"Good. Then I will begin," said the mayor in his deep, croaky, froggy voice. "Thank you for gathering here today. I have an important announcement that I think you will all find very exciting indeed."

"Ooh, I wonder what it will be!" whispered Blossom.

"I am delighted to tell you all that. . ." The mayor paused as everyone sat forward on their seats – "Jewel Forest is to host the next Fairy Olympics!"

Hearing these words, everyone in

Toadstool Town Hall cheered. The Fairy Olympics were held every four years – but Jewel Forest had never hosted them before. It was a *really* big deal.

"This is BRILLIANT!" cried Willa as she fluttered her wings in excitement.

"Oh, I can't wait!" added Catkin, clapping her hands. She turned to Pip. "You were right – it *is* something good!"

But although her friends were delighted, Pip wasn't so sure. The little fairy didn't really like sports – and she wasn't very good at them!

Ribbit! croaked the mayor as he tried to quieten the audience. "Now, creatures of the forest, there's a great deal of work to do! The Fairy Olympics will take place in just two days' time, so we'll need lots of help to get everything ready. And you'll need to practise for the events, as we'll have fairies visiting from all over fairyland to compete in our Olympics. We'll put on a fantastic show for the forest animals and creatures! There will be events designed especially for the forest: Toadstool Trampolining, Branch Gymnastics, River Rafting and Fairy Relay."

The mayor grinned and clapped his webbed hands together. "Right, that's all. Thank you, fairies! I know we're going to put on an Olympics like no other, and that you'll do Jewel Forest proud!"

Everyone began fluttering out of the hall. "You go on without me," Catkin told her friends. "I want to speak to the mayor about being on the organizing committee."

The fairies grinned – if there was one

thing Catkin loved to do above all else, it was organize!

The fairy friends waved goodbye to Catkin as they walked through the grand town hall entrance. Outside were two golden statues: one of a princess fairy and one of a hummingbird, showing the harmony between the fairies and creatures of the forest.

They emerged into the lush green forest, which sparkled in the afternoon sunshine. The jewels hanging from the trees glistened and the shiny leaves gleamed.

"I'm so looking forward to the Branch Gymnastics," said Blossom. "It's my favourite sport!"

The three fairies stepped on to the fairy skyway. The skyway was high above the forest ground and made of leafy bridges that connected the tree houses and shops. Shiny gems, dotted between the leaves, meant that it always glittered, even at night!

"I love Toadstool Trampolining!" said Willa. "I'm a bit rusty, but if I start practising right away, I hope I'll get the hang of it again quickly."

"Oh, and what about the River Rafting?" said Blossom, spinning round to face her friends. "It sounds like so much fun!"

The friends continued to chatter as they fluttered back home, although Pip was quiet. A niggling thought buzzed about her head: *What am I going to do? I really don't like sports!*

Get creative with the fashion fairy princesses in these magical sticker-activity books!

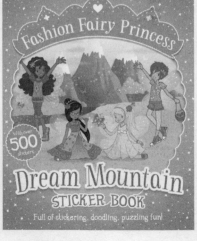